# Lacey O'Neal

Written by Arlen D. Cohn
Illustrated by Jeff Cole

If you drive out of town past the old swimming hole
past a fork in the road and eight telephone poles,
you'll find the most splendid, spectacular view
of the mountains and valleys around Camp Wazoo.

Every June parents pack up their kids and their gear
to attend Camp Wazoo as they do every year.
And most all of the kids were just like you and me—
except Lacey O'Neal—who stood almost six-three.

Lacey was happy above all the rest.
The view was just grand and the air was quite fresh.
She could see in a crowd what the others could not.
And she loved all the smiles and attention she got.

When a kite lost control in the breezes by chance
and got caught in the top of a Cottonwood branch,
it was Lacey that always appeared to help out.
'Cause she knew, after all, what good friends were about.

When the swim meet was held out on Camp Wazoo Lake
and Lacey was still in the frontrunner's wake,
there was never a doubt who would end in the lead,
because Lacey's long reach could beat anyone's speed.

When her friends would choose teams to go out and play hoops
she was first to be chosen to join the hoop groups.
When her team needed points it was quite a safe bet,
because Lacey was safe as a net bet could get.

Every camper liked Lacey, that is, except one.
He'd tease and he'd heckle and always poke fun.
He'd whine and complain more than all of the rest.
He was, without question, the Camp Wazoo pest.

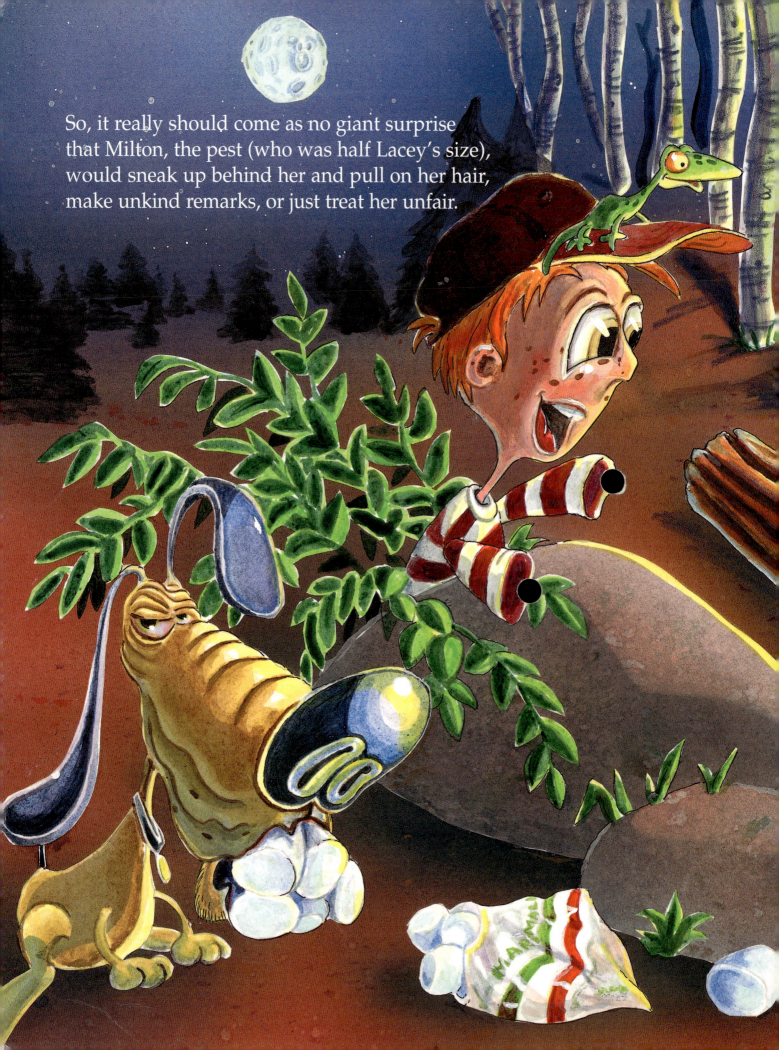

So, it really should come as no giant surprise
that Milton, the pest (who was half Lacey's size),
would sneak up behind her and pull on her hair,
make unkind remarks, or just treat her unfair.

One day the camp leaders divided up names
for the Camp Wazoo Yacht Club Canoe Racing Games.
Each team would canoe along South Wazoo Creek
for a chance to win ice cream and cake for a week.

Team one readied Lacey to row the canoe
against Milton who happened to be on team two.
As they raced through the course, Milton thought with a grin,
I know just what I'll do to make sure that I win.

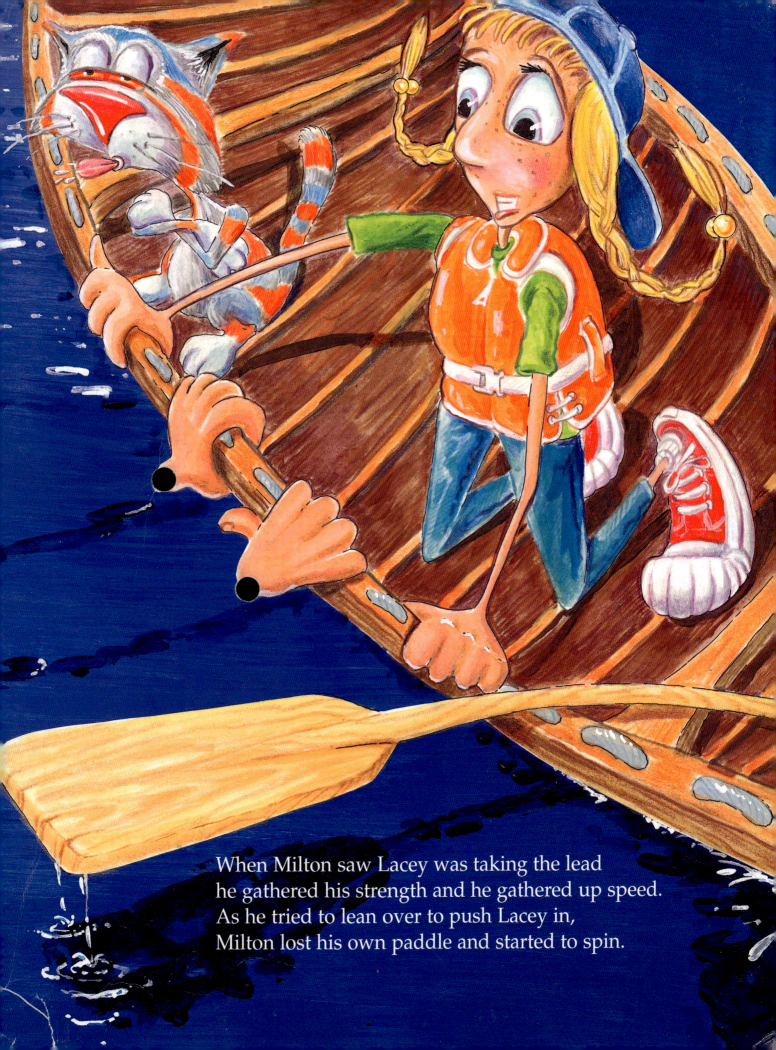

When Milton saw Lacey was taking the lead
he gathered his strength and he gathered up speed.
As he tried to lean over to push Lacey in,
Milton lost his own paddle and started to spin.

With no paddle to steer, Milton veered from the beach.
But nobody could grab him. They just couldn't reach.
There was only one chance to save Milton at all
before Milton's canoe hit Wazoo Waterfall.
That's when Lacey, the girl who stood almost six-three,
grabbed hold of his hand and pulled the lad free.

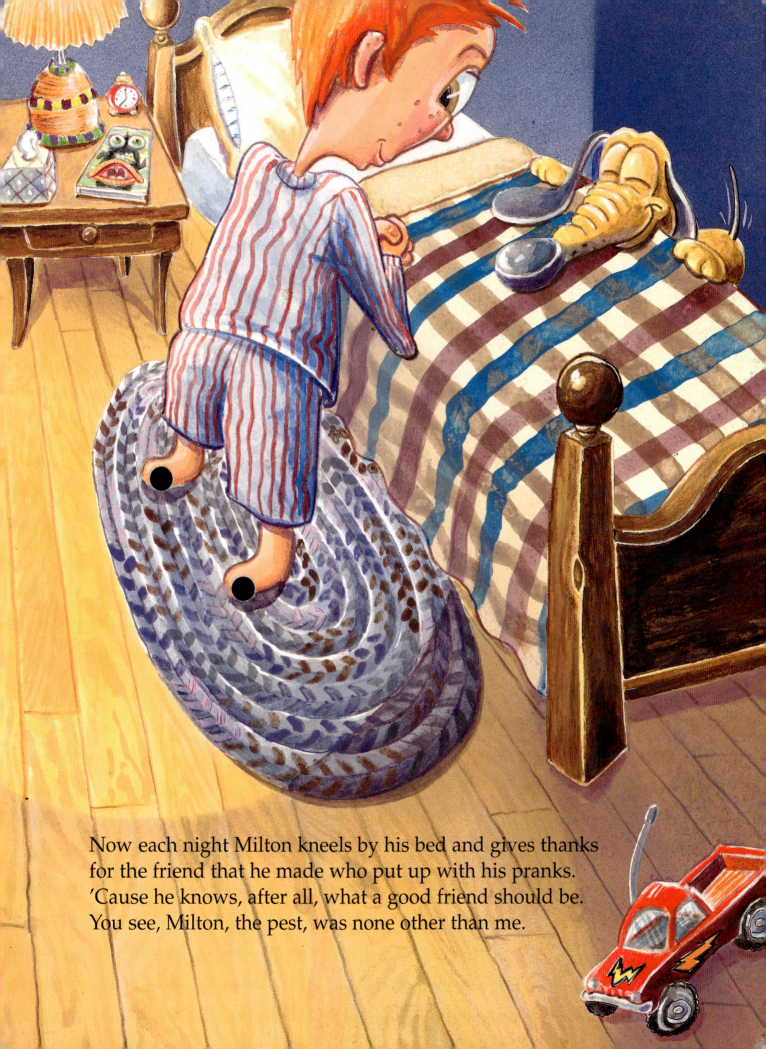

Now each night Milton kneels by his bed and gives thanks
for the friend that he made who put up with his pranks.
'Cause he knows, after all, what a good friend should be.
You see, Milton, the pest, was none other than me.

Shalom!
from Israel

Photo: Wernher Krutein/photovault.com

Ahalan!
from Egypt

Photo: Beverly Factor

Hola!
from Spain

Photo: Gary Kennedy

Yá' át' ééh!
from New Mexico, USA

Photo: Herbert Kaplan

Gia'sou!
from Greece

"Hello!" from Friends

around the World

G L O S

NORTH
AMERICA

Colorado
New Mexico

Central
America

Ecuador

SOUTH
AMERICA

Brazil

Hello!
from Colorado, USA

Photo: Heather Fleck

Ciao!
from Italy

Photo: Roger Stoller / photovault.com

Hola!
from Ecuador

Photo: Beverly Factor

Alo!
from Brazil

Photo: Mark Downey

G'day!
from Australia

Photo: PhotoLibrary of Australia

Hallo!
from the Netherlands